BIONICLE™

CHRONICLES #3

Makuta's Revenge

by C.A. Hapka

SCHOLASTIC INC.
New York Toronto London Auckland Sydney
Mexico City New Delhi Hong Kong Buenos Aires

ISBN 0-439-50119-9

Design by Peter Koblish

12 11 10 9 8   4 5 6 7 8/0

Printed in the U.S.A.
First printing, August 2003

The Legend of Mata Nui

In the time before time, the Great Spirit descended from the heavens, carrying we, the ones called the Matoran, to this island paradise. We were separate and without purpose, so the Great Spirit blessed us with three virtues: unity, duty, and destiny. We embraced these gifts and, in gratitude, we named our island home Mata Nui, after the Great Spirit himself.

But our happiness was not to last. Mata Nui's brother, Makuta, was jealous of these honors and betrayed him. Makuta cast a spell over Mata Nui, who fell into a deep slumber. Makuta's power dominated the land, as fields withered away, sunlight grew cold, and ancient values were forgotten.

Still, all hope was not lost. Legends told of six mighty heroes, the Toa, who would arrive to save Mata Nui. Time would reveal that these were not simply myths — for the Toa did appear on the shores of the island. They arrived with no memory, no knowledge of one another — but they pledged to defend Mata Nui and its people against the darkness. Tahu, Toa of Fire. Onua, Toa of Earth. Gali, Toa of Water. Lewa, Toa of Air. Pohatu, Toa of Stone. And Kopaka, Toa of Ice. Great warriors with great power, drawn from the very elements themselves. Together, they were six heroes with one destiny: to defeat Makuta and save Mata Nui.

This is their story.

UNDERGROUND

Deep beneath the island of Mata Nui, in a cavern so far below the surface that no ray of light had ever pierced its darkness, a pair of glowing red eyes stared out of a huge, shadowy face. Unblinking, the eyes turned upward, seeing far beyond what lay before them, through rock and earth and sand, all the way to the distant sunlit surface.

"Soooooooooo . . ." a deep, ominous voice breathed into the empty cave. "Toa. You have defeated the Bohrok swarms . . . as it was foreseen. And in doing so, you have called forth the instrument of your own doom."

The red eyes blinked and narrowed.

"And though the prophecies of the Matoran may sing of the Toa's might, we shall soon see that even the spirit of a hero can be broken." The dark voice sounded pleased. "The time has come — time to awaken the next protectors of Mata Nui's slumber. It is left to them to avenge the defeat of their Bohrok brothers. And to preserve things as they should be . . . as they must be . . . forever."

SYMBOLS AND SECRETS

"Look out below!"

Pohatu Nuva glanced up as he stepped out into the sandy main street of the desert village of Po-Koro. A hail of stone rained down from the wall that surrounded the village.

"Good job," he called to the workers atop the wall. "At this rate, you'll have this section of the wall repaired before sunset."

"Thank you for the kind words, Toa!" one of the workers called back.

Pohatu glanced at Turaga Onewa, the leader of the village, who had followed him outside. "They'd better be careful about calling me 'Toa' like that," he joked. "Especially when Toa Tahu is listening. It's supposed to be 'Toa Nuva' now."

Onewa chuckled. "Indeed," he agreed. "There have been a lot of changes on Mata Nui since you and the other Toa arrived."

"Yes." Pohatu looked down at himself, still a little amazed at the changes in his own body. It was stronger and sleeker than ever, with gleaming silver armor highlighting his bronze-and-gold limbs and torso. His mask had changed, too — instead of its old, smooth bulletlike shape, it was ridged and spiky and provided him with even stronger powers of speed.

There was another shout from the direction of the village wall. Pohatu and Onewa watched as several large, beetlelike creatures hauled a large chunk of stone toward the broken section. A villager pointed and called out, and the creatures obediently turned slightly to the left.

"Who would have thought it?" Pohatu said. "Not long ago we were fighting the Bohrok swarms. Now they're helping us repair the damage they caused."

"It is amazing indeed, Toa of Stone," Onewa agreed. "I must admit, I was not certain it was the right decision, letting the Bohrok swarms into the villages so soon after you and the other Toa defeated their queens."

"How could it be the wrong decision?" Pohatu said. "After all, it's one of the few things we six Toa have agreed upon since we arrived here."

It hadn't been long ago that he and the other Toa had first awakened on this island of Mata Nui. Even though the Toa were six heroes with one destiny, they didn't always find it easy to work together. But they had come together when it counted, most recently to defeat the Bohrok swarms sent by Makuta. In the end, the Toa had trapped the twin queens of the swarm, Cahdok and Gahdok — first with the help of the powerful Exo-Toa armor they had discovered in the queens' underground lair and then by releasing the mysterious substance known as protodermis. At the same time, the Toa were exposed to the protodermis themselves and emerged from it changed — into the Toa Nuva.

"Besides," Pohatu went on as he watched the Bohrok maneuver a square chunk of rock toward the wall, "we know now that it was the krana — the mysterious beings they carried within them — that controlled them. Now that the krana have been removed, there is no reason to fear the swarms anymore."

"Turaga! Turaga!" a shout interrupted their conversation. They turned to see a villager racing toward them.

"What is it, Hewkii?" Onewa asked as the Matoran skidded to a stop before them.

Hewkii gave a slight bow. "Forgive the interruption, Pohatu Nuva," he said. "But something extraordinary has just happened."

Pohatu and Onewa followed as Hewkii hurried back toward the center of the village. He led them to the village shrine known as the Po-Suva. A crowd of Po-Matoran had gathered there, clustered near the suva's entrance.

"Move aside!" Hewkii shouted. "Let the Toa Nuva and the Turaga see."

The villagers moved aside, murmuring with wonder. Pohatu saw a bronze-colored object hovering just above the ground.

"What is it?" he wondered aloud, taking a step forward. It was about the size of his mask, with carved lines forming an angular pattern in its smooth surface.

Turaga Onewa took in a sharp breath.

"What?" Pohatu glanced at him. "Do you know what that thing is?"

The Turaga frowned and began to tremble. "It is as it was foreseen . . ."

Tahu Nuva, the Toa of Fire, watched as Turaga Vakama set the strange object into a niche in the wall of the Ta-Suva, the village's sacred shrine.

"I still don't understand what it is," he said. "You say it's an icon — a symbol of my power. But what is its purpose? Where did it come from?"

"That cannot be said, Tahu Nuva," Vakama replied, bowing before the icon. "It is a mystery shrouded in the mists of the past."

"Yes," Tahu murmured with a twinge of an-noyance. "There seems to be a lot of those."

Tahu stepped outside the suva, but Vakama followed. "Tahu Nuva," he said. "Please come back inside for a moment. I have something of importance to discuss with you." Vakama drew the Toa back into the dark quiet of the suva. "I have been consulting with the Turaga of the other villages. We wanted to make sure you and the other Toa Nuva know that there is still work to be done — that becoming Toa Nuva does not end with your new looks and strength. There is a new set of Kanohi masks you must find to truly make use of all your new powers."

"New masks?" Tahu grimaced slightly. Soon after the Toa's arrival on Mata Nui, they had set out to find the sets of Kanohi masks that would give them great powers. They had been hidden all over the island, and Makuta had set his vicious minions, the Rahi, to guard them.

"It should not be such a difficult task this time," the Turaga said. "As you know, the Rahi no longer answer to Makuta. And with the Bohrok no longer a threat . . ."

". . . finding the masks should be as easy as a nice game of kolhii," Tahu finished. "All right. I suppose it's better to get this out of the way. Can you manage here without me for a while?"

"Of course," Vakama replied. "But . . ." His voice trailed off.

"Yes? What is it?" Tahu did his best to keep impatience out of his voice. "Is there something else?"

"There is." Vakama shifted his firestaff to the opposite hand. "I — I don't know if the time is right. I don't know if any time would be right for this. And the wrong decision . . ."

"Yes, what are you saying?" Tahu demanded. It wasn't like Vakama to sound so hesitant. The Turaga was usually much more like Tahu himself — quick-thinking and decisive. "What's the big secret?"

Taking a deep breath, Vakama reached into an opening in the wall and pulled something out.

Tahu stared at the item curiously. "What is that?" he asked, reaching toward it. "It looks sort of like a mask — but not any mask I've ever seen."

Vakama held up the object. Its surface gleamed a deep flame orange.

"It *is* a mask," Vakama said, his voice low and reverent. "The Kanohi Vahi — the Great Mask of Time. It is the most powerful mask of them all."

"Really?" Tahu reached out eagerly.

But Vakama pulled it out of reach. "Wait," he said, his voice so serious and commanding that Tahu lowered his hand in surprise. "You must understand what this power means."

Tahu frowned, irritated. "I am a Toa Nuva," he reminded Vakama haughtily. "I know all about the use of power."

Still, Vakama held the Vahi mask away. He shook his head. "This is not the kind of power you have known," he said. "Your other powers are great indeed. But the power of the Vahi exists on a higher level. Do you understand what it would mean to control time itself?"

Tahu paused, turning over the question in his head. "I — I suppose it would be useful in battle," he said. "I could slow down time for my opponent, giving me the chance to defeat him before he could even complete a strike. Or I could use it instead of the mask of speed, quickening time to get me somewhere faster. Or . . ."

"No!" Vakama sighed. "This is what I feared. You must think of the greater reality, Toa Tahu. For he who controls time controls reality — controls *everything*. Do you see?"

"I see that time connects all other powers," Tahu said slowly. "Nothing else can exist without it."

"Yes!" Vakama sounded pleased and relieved, though his voice still held an undercurrent of worry. "Now you begin to understand. It's one thing to control time and with it all of reality — and another to *lose* control of it all. The Kanohi Vahi can only be used in the direst emergency — when there is nothing to lose."

Tahu paused. "But, I might never reach such a state of desperation at all," he said. "I might never find a chance to call upon the Vahi."

"That is my hope," Vakama said. "In fact, I think it would be better if the other Toa never know you hold it unless you need to use it. Can you accept that, Tahu Nuva?"

Tahu thought for a moment, struggling with the idea. To have the most powerful mask of all and never to use it . . . never to let on that it existed . . . Could he really maintain such a secret?

"Why me?" he blurted. "Why should I be the one to be given this responsibility?"

"Why does anything on Mata Nui happen as it does?" Vakama responded. "We cannot know. We can only accept our destiny."

Tahu sighed. Unity, duty, destiny — such were the ideas the Matoran lived by. He glanced at Vakama, who was watching him carefully. How much did Vakama and the other Turaga really know about the Toa's destiny? He wondered. Did they see more of the future and the past than they told?

"All right," he said at last. "I will do my best to protect this mask — and its secrets."

He reached again for the Kanohi Vahi. And this time Vakama allowed him to take it.

PRIDE AND POWER

"Don't be late, don't be late," Lewa Nuva, Toa of Air, sang to himself as he launched himself off of a cliff near the edge of Le-Wahi.

Don't be late. It was the last thing Toa Onua had said to him when the six Toa Nuva had parted ways.

The other five Toa Nuva were waiting when Lewa finally reached the meeting spot. Gali smiled at him, and Pohatu gave a friendly wave.

"Greetings, brothers," Lewa called. "And sister," he added with a wink at Gali, the Toa of Water. "Did I latemiss anything important?"

Onua, the Toa of Earth, greeted him with a nod. "We have just recently arrived ourselves. But how are things in Le-Koro, brother?" he asked in his deep, rumbling voice. "We have all wondered."

Lewa's smile faded as he thought of the rubble that was all that had remained of his tree-bright village after the Bohrok got through with it. If only he had fought harder to resist the power of that krana . . . He shuddered as he remembered the horrible feeling that had come over him when one of the krana had taken over his mind.

He shook his head, refusing to dwell any longer on such things. The past was past, and even a Toa could not change time.

"We are hardworking," he said. "There is much to do, but we are making progress."

"That is good to hear, Lewa," Gali said. "Let us know if you are in need of our help."

Lewa shrugged. "Manythanks, Gali," he replied. "But with my new powers, I truedoubt I will need much help with anything."

"Indeed." It was always a surprise when Kopaka Nuva, the Toa of Ice, had anything to say. But now his cool voice cut into the conversation. "I fail to see why any of us need to bother with these meetings any longer. Not until we discover how to awaken Mata Nui." It was the Toa's ultimate goal to reawaken the Great Spirit for whom the island had been named.

"Let's not be hasty, brother Kopaka," Gali said. "Even our new power doesn't mean we can go it alone from here on in."

"Oh, really? Watch this." Lewa flung his katana blade upward, calling upon the power of the wind. It swept down with a roar, lifting the other Toa Nuva off their feet.

"Take care where you point that power of yours, brother Lewa," Tahu Nuva growled as he leaped to his feet. "You might just find yourself in hot water. . . ." He sent a blast of flame out of his magma sword.

Lewa somersaulted out of the way just in time. "Is that the best you can do, Tahu Nuva?"

Before long all of the Toa Nuva had joined in, each trying to overwhelm the others with a show of his or her new powers. Pohatu unleashed a tornado of stones. Onua started an avalanche on a nearby slope. Tahu and Kopaka battled with their opposing powers of heat and cold. Even Gali sent a mighty flood gushing out from her new aqua axes.

Finally, though, the Toa Nuva lost interest in the game. "Well, that was fun," Pohatu said breathlessly. "What will we do for an encore?"

Gali looked sheepish. "As Toa Nuva, we have greater control than ever before," she said. "It is a shame we cannot control our tempers as well."

"We are all on edge, Gali," Pohatu said soothingly. "The struggle with Cahdok and Gahdok — our transformation into the Toa Nuva . . ."

"Not to mention rebuilding our villages," Lewa added, his mind wandering back to Le-Koro. His hands quivered slightly, impatient to get back to work helping with the repairs.

"Maybe it would be best for us to go our separate ways for now," Tahu put in. "Our villages need us more than we need one another."

"I agree," Kopaka said. "This alliance is no longer necessary."

Gali looked dismayed. "Split apart — again? Have we learned nothing from the past?"

Lewa shrugged. He liked Gali, but in his

opinion she had always put a little too much emphasis on the *unity* part of the Matoran's favorite saying, even when it didn't seem necessary.

"This is a mistake," Gali pleaded. "I can feel it. Please — what if we are needed once more? What if some new danger threatens Mata Nui?"

"We will tug that vine when we come to it, watersister," Lewa called over his shoulder. "Quickspeed to you — I am out of here."

Soon Lewa was sailing in for a landing on the outskirts of the village. He could see that the Matoran had made progress even in the short time he'd been away.

There was a crashing sound in the brush nearby. Lewa glanced toward it, expecting to see an animal. Instead, a Tahnok Va — a scout of the fiery Tahnok breed of Bohrok — emerged.

News . . . news ahead.

The thought slipped easily into Lewa's mind. He shuddered slightly. Because of his experience with the krana, Lewa was the only Toa who could hear and understand the Bohrok's communication. He still couldn't quite get used to the fact that the swarms still had access to his mind, though it had certainly come in handy.

"What news?" he asked the Tahnok Va, ignoring his own uneasy feelings. "What's happening? Is something badwrong at the village?"

No . . . no . . . nothing wrong . . .

With that, the Tahnok Va turned and scurried away into the jungle. Lewa frowned after it for a moment. Nothing wrong — he hoped that was true. It was still hard to trust the Bohrok sometimes after all that had happened.

Whatever the news, Lewa figured he would know soon enough. He grabbed the closest vine and swung upward. "I'm back, little ones," he called as he landed.

He need not have bothered. The entire population of the village was already gathered nearby. The Le-Matoran let out a cheer.

"Welcome back, Toa," Turaga Matau called. "We've been waiting for you. We just finished repairing your suva and we can finally put your power icon in its proper place in the heart of the village."

Lewa nodded. He had nearly forgotten about the strange floating symbol that had appeared out of nowhere earlier that day.

"And don't forget the celebration!" a voice shouted from the crowd.

"A celebration?" Lewa said. "What are we waiting for? Let's get started!"

A cheer rang out from the gathered villagers. Soon someone was playing a lively tune on a Madu-shell xylophone, and Matoran were dancing, leaping, and swinging playfully on nearby vines.

Turaga Matau put a hand on Lewa's arm. "Before you join the party, would you like to see the suva?" he asked.

"Sure," Lewa replied. He followed the Turaga toward a mound-shaped structure at the center of the village.

Inside, the woven walls allowed only a dim glow of soothing green light to seep in from outside. At the center of the small, round room was a solid stone shelf.

A niche had been cut into the stone. Resting in it was the symbol.

Lewa gazed at it curiously. It was square and intricately carved out of a greenish stonelike substance. Where had it come from? What did it mean?

He didn't wonder about it for long. "Very nice," he told the Turaga. "But enough symbolgazing. Let's get out there and have some partyfun!"

Soon he and Matau had rejoined the gleeful crowd on the platform. As he danced and laughed along with his villagers, Lewa could feel some of the tension of the recent battles draining away.

If only stuffy old Kopaka could see us now! Lewa thought with a grin. *Or any of the others, for that factmatter. Nobody knows how to have restfun like a Le-Matoran!*

Overwhelmed by joy, Lewa shouted for attention. "Watch this, leafbrothers," he cried, balancing on the edge of the platform. "I'll show you the kind of sunsoaring I can do with my new powers!"

He crouched briefly, then sprang up, putting all of his energy into the leap. Up, up, up . . .

he soared straight into the sky above the tree-tops, higher and higher until he was almost blinded by the bright light of the sun.

"Yeee-haaaa!" he cried as he reached the top of the arc.

He waved his hand, calling upon the air currents to carry him down. As he did, he glanced down. He was a bit startled by how high he was.

"Good thing my friend the wind is always ready to do my bidding," Lewa murmured. Realizing the breeze he'd summoned hadn't yet materialized, he swirled his hand in the air again.

Still the wind didn't respond.

"What?" Lewa cried, his heart clenching with fear as he tried again — and again. He felt himself plummeting downward as he realized the truth — his elemental powers had deserted him.

He tumbled helplessly down toward the village far — *too* far — below.

THE THEFT

"*KRAAA!*"

Lewa's eyes flew open. He realized he had closed them to shut out the view of the hard ground rushing toward him. "Oof!" he cried as his descent was suddenly stopped just above the ground.

For a second all he could see was a feathery neck. He clung to it, realizing he was still moving downward — but at a much safer speed.

"Are you okay, Toa?" a breathless voice asked.

"Kongu?" Lewa said. "Is that you?"

"It's me and Ka," the Matoran responded. "It looked like you were in troublebad, so we up-flew to check."

"Thank you, bravebrother," Lewa said as he finally realized it was the beating wings and strong body of Ka the Gukko that had stopped his free fall. He glanced at Kongu, who was perched on the large bird's back. "I — I know not what wrong happened, but the wind didn't answer my herecall."

With a squawk, Ka glided in for a landing, depositing Lewa on the swampy ground.

"What do you mean, Toa?" Kongu asked. "How could the airwind not respond to you?"

Lewa shook his head. "I don't know, little brother," he said. "It has not happened before."

Not wanting to think about it anymore just then, he grabbed a vine and swung up into the village. Kongu followed aboard Ka.

As he landed on the main platform, Lewa saw that the villagers were clustered together, their eyes and voices full of fear.

"Don't worryfret, little ones," he called, assuming that they were concerned for his safety. "I'm all right."

Matau rushed up to him, his eyes wild and

frightened. "I'm gladhearted to hear that, Toa," he said. "But I'm afraid there is other wrongnews. Your power icon has been stolen!"

"This creature," Onua Nuva said patiently, "what did it look like?"

The Onu-Matoran standing before him, a sturdy villager named Onepu, bowed his head. "It was large," he reported. "But I prepared to fight it."

Onua nodded. "Go on."

"I — I know not how else to describe it," Onepu said, his voice shaking slightly. "It was hideous — terrifying. Its body had a metallic sheen, and its claws were huge. I shouted for help, knowing I could not hold it off for long on my own. Then it — it spoke to me."

He was silent for a long moment. Onua waited, gathering his patience.

Finally Onepu continued. "Its words were as metallic and cold as its body," he said, his voice twisted with horror. "It told me to step aside so that it might claim its prize. When I would not, it — it began to breathe in. Within seconds, it had sucked away all of the air within the suva. I tried to hold my post, but with no air I found myself helpless. It pushed past me and grabbed the icon — and then it was gone."

Onua turned the story over and over in his mind. Who was this new, mysterious enemy with such strange and disturbing powers? What did it want with Onua's power symbol?

"What does it mean, Toa?" Onepu asked meekly. "Why did it happen?"

"I thought these icons were merely that — symbols of we Toa's elemental powers, artistic tributes to our destiny," Onua said slowly, allowing the careful logic of his thoughts to unfold aloud. "But now I see that the icons actually held these powers within them. As long as my icon remained in the village, my power remained strong. Now that the symbol is gone, so are my powers."

It was an uncomfortable feeling. Onua was accustomed to being the strongest of the strong. Now he was left helpless — and it seemed that a powerful new enemy had appeared on Mata Nui.

Just when we thought Makuta's forces were stamped out for good . . . Onua thought. He recalled Gali's words earlier that day. As usual, she had been right — she had been the only one with the wisdom to realize that Makuta would not be finished with them yet.

"What should we do now?" Onepu asked. "Should I call out the Ussal forces and go after the thief?"

"Not just yet," Onua said. "Go tell the Turaga what has happened. I'd better check in with the other Toa Nuva. Together we will decide what to do."

THE CHASE

Kopaka Nuva glided slowly down the snowy slope, reminding himself to be careful. While he could still ski, he no longer had the ability to control the ice beneath his feet. That skill had deserted him along with all the rest of them.

It's beginning to seem that Gali's earlier worries were well-founded, he thought bleakly. *Our split seemed almost too easy this time. As if it were destined to happen — or as if someone or something wanted it to happen.*

He still couldn't believe that his elemental powers had suddenly deserted him. It was only thanks to his determination — and the help of Turaga Nuju — that he had survived his sudden tumble off of a crumbling ice bridge.

As soon as he heard that the Ice Toa's powers were gone, the Turaga had suggested that Kopaka seek out the others. If it had happened to all of them . . . Well, there was no telling what might become of Mata Nui in that case.

Before long Kopaka left the snow behind and climbed down to the Toa's usual meeting place. To his relief, both Pohatu Nuva and Tahu Nuva were waiting for him in the clearing.

"I guess this means the icon thief has struck in Ko-Koro, too, ice brother," Pohatu said by way of greeting.

Kopaka nodded.

"Whoever or whatever this foe may be, it will regret stealing our powers!" Tahu raged. "I will make sure of that!" He raised his magma sword for emphasis. Instead of its usual flickering flame, the sword merely smoked weakly.

"Anger will not help us," Kopaka pointed out. "We need to unite, to form a plan."

Tahu let out a short, disbelieving laugh. "Has the thief stolen my hearing as well?" he exclaimed. "I would swear I just heard Kopaka, the Toa of Doing His Own Thing, suggest that we unite!"

"Brothers, brothers," Pohatu pleaded. "Enough with the petty disagreements. We have enough problems without that. Let's try to work together here, okay?"

"Good advice at any time." Onua Nuva's voice interrupted the tense moment. He strode into the clearing and glanced around. "But especially important now, I think. All of you — you've lost your elemental powers, too?"

Each Toa nodded. "I think it's safe to assume that Gali and Lewa will have been struck as well," Pohatu added.

"You're right about that," Lewa said, hurrying into the clearing just in time to respond. "Found that out in a wrongmoment back in Le-Koro."

Onua nodded. "Then we need to decide what to do."

"I know what to do," Tahu spoke up at once. "Find the thief and take the symbols back. End of plan."

Kopaka sighed. Typical Tahu — all bluster with no thought. "That's no plan," he said icily. "That's suicide."

"Kopaka is right," Pohatu agreed. "Without our powers, and knowing not what we might be facing, it would be foolish to rush into action."

"Who are you calling foolish?" Tahu snapped, glaring from Pohatu to Kopaka and back again.

Onua raised his hand. "Easy, brother Tahu," he said. "Let's just think on this for a moment."

Lewa rolled his eyes behind his mask. "Yes, a moment," he quipped. "Or a day, or a month. With all due respect, brother Onua, if we spent as much time wait-thinking as you would like, we'd never get anything done at all."

Kopaka winced as Onua frowned. Lewa often spoke without thinking, but rarely did he purposely insult anyone. It was clear that the loss of powers was setting all of them on edge. *Where is sister Gali?* he wondered. *She's usually the only one who can make peace at such a moment.*

As if responding to his thought, Gali raced into the clearing at that very moment. "Brothers!" she cried breathlessly. "Good, you're all here. I have news!"

"We know," Pohatu said. "Symbol stolen, powers gone, blah blah blah. Old news."

Gali shook her head. "Not that," she said. "I already heard from a messenger that the thief struck all of us. Or, rather, the *thieves*."

"There is more than one creature stealing our powers?" Onua asked.

"Yes," Gali replied, leaning on her aqua ax for support as she caught her breath. "My village guards were as helpless as yours before the intruder — it disabled them by filling the suva with electricity that pinned them to the walls. But others saw what happened and followed — and tracked it to the edge of Po-Wahi, where they saw it join with two others like it."

"What are we waiting for?" Tahu hoisted his sword. "Let's get to Po-Wahi!"

"Wait!" Onua cried. But Tahu had already charged off, with Lewa right behind him. Even Pohatu trotted after them eagerly.

"Reckless fools," Kopaka muttered.

Gali glanced at him. "I agree, some of our brothers could stand to do a little more thinking before they act," she said. "But this time, their course might be the best one. The longer we are without our powers, the greater the danger to Mata Nui. We have to confront these creatures and take back our icons."

"I suppose you are right, sister," Onua said, his voice deep with worry. "But how easy will it be to do so without our powers?"

Kopaka was wondering the same thing. But he followed without another word as Gali and Onua hurried after the others.

Soon the six Toa Nuva were moving as a group through the open, rocky pass between the northern section of Le-Wahi and the eastern slopes of Mount Ihu.

"We should at least try to be prepared for what we will face when we find the thieves," Onua pointed out as he hurried along near the back of the group. "The least we can do is share what information we have. What did your Matoran see? What tools did the creatures use against them?"

Each Toa Nuva described everything he or

she knew in turn. Tahu reported that the creature in his village had disabled the guards with a wall of intense sound so loud that it had cracked the walls of the suva. The creature that had stolen Lewa's icon had used a strong magnetic force to push away the Le-Matoran. In Onua's village, the weapon of choice had been a vacuum power that had sucked all of the air out of the suva. Pohatu had lost his symbol to a creature that had thrown off such intense heat that everything around it turned instantly to plasma. And Gali had already mentioned the electricity used against her villagers.

When his turn came, Kopaka briefly described the way one of the creatures had affected gravity, making the Ko-Matoran guard's limbs and body too heavy to move. "It sounds like there may be six separate attackers, not three," he finished. "Six enemies, and six of us."

"Three or six, three dozen or six hundred, it matters not," Tahu said with a shrug. "We must face them down no matter what."

With that, he hurried forward to the end

of the pass. Beyond lay the open, sweeping vista of the great northern desert.

"Now which waypath do we take?" Lewa wondered.

Onua pointed. "I would say we go that way."

Kopaka followed the Earth Toa's glance and saw broad prints leading northward in the bare soil. The marks were large and deep.

"Come on!" Tahu said. "Are we going to stand around looking at these tracks, or are we going to follow them and take back what is ours?"

Without waiting for an answer, he strode off in the direction the tracks led.

"Our enemies seem to be making no attempt to remain stealthy," Pohatu commented. "I wonder if we should be worried by that."

"They should be worried about us!" Tahu said boldly. He led the way over a rise. Beyond lay a large, rocky plain scattered with stones of all shapes and sizes.

"Does anyone see prints?" Gali asked.

Pohatu shook his head. "It will be pointless

trying to find them here," he said. "This sort of ground is not friendly to ordinary tracking."

"Maybe we should go back," Onua said. "We could seek out the rest of the Kanohi Nuva — with those additional powers, it may be easier to find the thieves."

"We've got to continue on." Tahu seemed unwilling to accept reality. "If we search Po-Wahi, we have to catch up to them."

"Or maybe not, if they've pathchanged to the tunnels of Onu-Wahi or anywhere else." Lewa shrugged. "Besides, what do we do if we find them?"

Kopaka grimaced. Where had that question been when they were all back at the meeting place?

"It's not 'if,'" Tahu said, breaking into Kopaka's thoughts. "We *will* find them, and we *will* get our powers back."

Pohatu was still staring across the rocky plain. Now he raised his hand and pointed. "Uh, Tahu?" he said. "I think those things up ahead might have something to say about it."

HELPLESS

Pohatu stared as the six creatures he had spotted came closer. Their bodies were sinewy and powerful-looking, covered in gleaming metallic armor of various shades — red, blue, silver, bronze, green, and black.

"What *are* those things?" Onua murmured.

"They look sort of like Bohrok," Pohatu said. "Only meaner."

Gali grimaced. "Let's just hope there aren't swarms of them somewhere," she commented. "These six look to be enough to deal with."

"And deal with them we will," Tahu said grimly, tightening his grip on his magma sword.

By then the creatures had nearly reached the Toa Nuva. One of them, the one with the reddish-colored armor, stepped forward.

"We are the Bohrok-Kal," it announced in a hard, smooth voice. "We search for Cahdok and Gahdok, queens of the swarms."

Pohatu's eyes widened in surprise. The queens? So he had been right — these must be a strange sort of Bohrok. The original swarms had been controlled by the queens. But these creatures seemed to function all on their own.

"Tell us where you have hidden the Bahrag, and then stand aside. We have no wish to harm helpless foes."

"Helpless?" Lewa exclaimed, charging forward. "Toa Nuva are never helpless!"

The Bohrok-Kal raised its greenish metal shield. "No amount of speed can save you from my magnetic force," it said coldly as a wave of power rippled out from the shield's surface.

Lewa was stopped in place so quickly that he nearly toppled over. "My feet!" Lewa cried. "Magnetized to the ground! I can't move!"

Onua grabbed an enormous boulder and lifted it above his head. Even without his elemental powers, his strength remained awesome.

Before he could throw the boulder, another Bohrok-Kal lifted its shield and sent a wave of concentrated power toward it. "Your rock is no threat, Toa Nuva," the creature said as the boulder dissolved into magma. "And neither are you. Give us Cahdok and Gahdok — now!"

Tahu leaped toward Gali, Pohatu, and Kopaka. His mask was glowing brightly.

"The Mask of Shielding will protect us for now," Tahu said as his mask's force field surrounded himself and the other three Toa. "Bohrok-Kal, your quest must fail — the creatures you seek have vanished from Mata Nui."

"You lie!" the black Bohrok-Kal hissed. "They are here and we will find them. Your shield cannot stand before the crushing power of gravity, Tahu Nuva."

A second later Tahu hit the ground hard. Gali gasped as she saw him struggling to lift his sword. His weight, multiplied a hundredfold by the Bohrok-Kal's gravity power, crushed the stones beneath it as he sank into the ground.

"Tahu!" Gali cried, horrified to see the bold and powerful Fire Toa made so helpless.

"The shield is down," Kopaka said grimly. "Defend yourselves, Toa Nuva!"

"There can be no defense against Tahnok-Kal's electricity," the reddish Bohrok-Kal said.

"Or Kohrak-Kal's sonic power," the silvery one hissed.

"And Lehvak-Kal's vacuum blast," the greenish creature added.

Gali gulped. A second later, she felt herself flung backward by a blast of combined energy so strong that she could hardly tell where one force ended and the next began. Air, electricity, sound — all surrounded and overwhelmed her, filling her mind and body so that, for a long moment, they seemed to cease to exist.

THE SEARCH

Tahu opened his eyes and sat up, unsure how much time had passed. There was no sign of the Bohrok-Kal anywhere.

Beside him, Lewa began to stir. "Ugh," he said blearily. "What happened?"

"I believe we have just been given a warning by the Bohrok-Kal," Onua said heavily, pushing himself upright. "They obviously do not want us interfering with their search."

Tahu scowled. "No?" he cried, jumping to his feet. "Well, the Bohrok-Kal will pay for daring to challenge the Toa Nuva. We shall —"

"Tahu!" Gali cut him off. By this time all six Toa were awake, sitting up and testing their limbs for injury. "This is no time to worry about our pride. If they find Cahdok and Gahdok and free them, the Bohrok swarms will strike again!"

"But how do we stop them?" Pohatu sounded worried. "Our powers are gone."

Tahu noticed that Lewa's eyes were clouded and his expression slightly pained. "What is it, brother?" he asked with concern. "Are you hurt?"

Lewa shook his head. "No, it's not that," he said. "It's just . . ." His voice trailed off hesitantly.

"What?" Tahu asked sharply, not liking the look in Lewa's eyes. It reminded him of the way the Air Toa had looked after being taken over by the Bohrok swarms. "Tell us what's wrong." It was an order, not a suggestion.

"Fine, fine," Lewa said. "Don't get your swords in a muddletwist. I — I could be dream-thinking it from the blow. But I thought I heard something. From the Bohrok-Kal."

"Heard something?" Gali repeated with interest. "What do you mean?"

Lewa shrugged. "Communication. Thought-talk," he said. "Like that of the krana."

Pohatu blinked in surprise. "Are you saying

there are krana inside these Bohrok-Kal, controlling them, just as there were in the Bohrok?"

"That would make sense," Kopaka pointed out. "These Bohrok-Kal seem to be related to the Bohrok somehow. They share the same goal."

"Not exactly," Gali said. "After all, Bohrok-Kal don't seem interested in damaging anything. They left the villages untouched."

"They're trying to frighten us," Lewa said. "To make us run so we won't try to stop them."

Kopaka scowled. "No one makes me run," he said coldly. "No one."

For once, Tahu agreed with the Ice Toa. "Enough talk," he said. "Gali, you, Pohatu, and Onua go back to the Bohrok nest — see if you can discover what happened to Cahdok and Gahdok. Kopaka, Lewa, and I will keep after the Bohrok-Kal — see if we can slow them down."

"I suggest we all keep our eyes out for Kanohi Nuva masks," Onua said as he joined Gali and Pohatu. "With our elemental energies gone, we need all the help we can get."

*   *   *

Onua was troubled as he followed Gali and Po-hatu, heading for the entrance to the Bahrag's nest. *How are we supposed to do it?* he thought uneasily. *How are we supposed to fulfill our destiny to protect Mata Nui when our greatest powers have been taken from us?*

Gali glanced over her shoulder at him. "This is a momentous challenge that we face, brother," she commented. "Perhaps the greatest test yet of our resolve."

Shading his eyes against the glare of the sun, Onua smiled at her. He had often noticed that the Toa of Water could all but read others' thoughts at times.

"Yes," he agreed. "It will not be easy. But we cannot falter. All of Mata Nui depends on us."

"The weakness this time may lie in the krana-kal," Gali pointed out. "They could be controlling the Bohrok-Kal just as the krana controlled the regular swarms."

Onua nodded. "I was thinking about that, too," he said. "I hope brother Lewa is right about hearing krana voices. It could be our only hope."

"I suppose so," Pohatu said. "If we can fig-ure out a way to separate the krana-kal from the Bohrok-Kal, we just might —"

"Hush," Onua broke in, picking up a sound from somewhere up ahead.

A second later, something large and fast-moving crashed into sight from around a bend in the riverbed. It was the reddish-colored Bohrok-Kal, the one known as the Tahnok-Kal.

"Stand aside, Toa Nuva," it hissed loudly as it came. "You are in my way."

"We will not," Pohatu said boldly. "If you want to go this way, you'll have to go through us."

Onua stepped up beside him, as did Gali. The Tahnok-Kal didn't slow its pace. It merely raised its shield, sending several lightning bolts shooting out of it.

"Look out!" Gali shouted, but it was too late. The bolts hit the ground beneath Onua, flinging him into the air, where he tumbled over and over before landing with a heavy thud on the bank of the dry river.

"Oof!" Pohatu grunted as he landed beside

him a second later. Nearby, Gali dropped heavily onto the hard-packed ground as well.

Onua blinked, trying to clear his mind. Pushing himself upright, he looked down into the riverbed just in time to see the Tahnok-Kal hurrying on without a backward glance.

The Toa of Earth squinted, willing his sun-weakened eyes to focus. "Look," he croaked, pointing. "Is that . . . ?"

The other two followed his gaze. Gali gasped. "A krana-kal!" she said. "The creature carries it beneath its face shield. So Lewa *was* right!"

Pohatu stared after the Tahnok-Kal as it disappeared around a bend. "That thing," he said, sounding shaken. "It didn't even slow down! It just knocked us aside and kept going."

Gali climbed to her feet. "Come on, brothers," she said wearily. "The only good news is that the Tahnok-Kal was heading away from the tunnel entrance. We'd better take advantage and get there before it does."

Soon the three of them were hurrying up a rocky slope. At the top, Onua knew they would find the entrance, buried under a giant pile of rocks. After their battle with the Bohrok queens, an avalanche had completely covered the opening.

Pohatu was already moving forward toward the pile of rocks. He drew back one foot and kicked at a large boulder.

"Ow!" he shouted as his foot connected with the solid stone. The boulder didn't budge.

"Pohatu, don't," Gali said gently. "Without your powers, you'll only wear yourself out."

Onua sighed. "We're going to have to find a different way," he said.

Gali stared at the covered cave entrance. "I'm starting to think that seeking out the Bahrag ourselves is a waste of time," she said. "It's unlikely we would be able to stop the Bohrok-Kal from getting to them anyway. I think we should focus instead on finding a way to get those krana-kal. Without them, the Bohrok-Kal will most likely be left directionless — and harmless."

"I agree," Onua said. "We need to get those krana-kal — any way we can."

THE SOUNDSHAPE

"Easy, easy," Lewa Nuva murmured under his breath. "Don't look uptree, my metallic friend. Nothing to see up here . . ."

He carefully swung across a clearing on a vine, his gaze trained on the Kohrok-Kal, which was marching along the ground below. The creature seemed unaware of the Toa Nuva's presence.

He hadn't kept track of how much time had passed since that first meeting with the Bohrok-Kal, but it seemed like forever. The Toa had split up, trying to get the Krana-Kal. But every encounter had ended the same way — with the Toa Nuva groaning on the ground while the Bohrok-Kal continued their quest without so much as a pause.

At least we found a fewnumber of Kanohi masks along the way, Lewa thought, trying to look on the bright side. *So we each have some of our maskpowers back now.*

Below, the Kohrak-Kal moved on. *Just a few farthersteps,* Lewa thought, willing himself to be patient. *It's almost time.*

He grasped a strong vine hanging nearby, glancing up to make sure that it was firmly en-twined around a higher branch.

When the creature was near the middle of the clearing, Lewa nodded. It was time.

He bent his knees and pushed off, springing gracefully off the tree branch. Holding the vine tightly with one hand, he held the other out-stretched at the ready. The vine swung him down, down, down — as the vine's arc reached the clearing, he was skimming just above the swampy ground.

Perfect! he thought eagerly, aiming straight toward the Kohrok-Kal. The creature's broad back was to him, and Lewa could clearly see the softly glowing white krana-kal set into the center of it. He was almost close enough to grab it . . .

WHANNNNNNNNNG!

A burst of noise exploded out of the Kohrok-Kal just as Lewa reached it, knocking him to the ground as solidly as any physical strike might do. Lewa was momentarily stunned by the blow, but quickly leaped to his feet. The Kohrak-Kal hardly spared him a glance as it continued easily on its way, but it did gesture briefly in his direction with its shield. A split second later, a high wall of solid sound sprang up between it and the Toa Nuva — vibrating and whining, sending leaves scattering away and causing tree trunks at the edge of the clearing to bend and crack.

"You won't awayblock the Toa of Air so easily," Lewa muttered, though his words were lost in the cacophony. Taking a deep breath, he called upon the power of the Mask of Levitation. He floated upward, easily reaching the top of the wall.

As soon as he did, the sonic waves shifted slightly, moving out and around him and blocking his rise. The wall of sound surrounded him, pummeling him with its intensity, so loud that it seemed it would crack the earth and sky themselves.

Lewa dropped back to the ground, hardly noticing the force of the fall. Much worse was the force of the sound assaulting his ears — staggering, inconceivable sound. How could any creature hold such terrible power?

Lewa couldn't think, couldn't move — could do nothing but try to survive the assault.

It was unbearable — like nothing he had ever experienced, like nothing he could ever have imagined. It bent his mind until it could think no more, his body until it could stand against it no more.

"Kopaka!" Gali's voice was urgent. "Come here — quick!"

Kopaka abandoned the Bohrok-Kal footprint he was examining and hurried forward to join Gali, who had moved several lengths ahead through the jungle.

"The soundshape . . . the soundshape . . ."

Lewa was muttering, his gaze blank and his limbs curled into a fetal position.

"Lewa!" Kopaka said sharply. "Brother Lewa, do you hear me?"

"He's in shock," Gali said, kneeling beside the Toa of Air. "Give him a moment."

Kopaka nodded, watching as Lewa writhed on the ground. Mud and swampy water covered him, making it clear that he'd been there quite a while. What could have happened to him?

The Bohrok-Kal, of course, Kopaka told himself grimly. *Our foolish airheaded brother must have decided to try to take one on by himself. Hasn't he learned his lesson by now?*

Kopaka noticed that the Toa of Air was pressing his hands to his ears. "Look at that," he told Gali. "He must have tangled with the sonic shield of the Kohrak-Kal."

"Yes," Gali agreed with a shudder. "That one is worse than all the others combined, if you ask me."

She reached down and gently tried to pry one of Lewa's hands loose. He struggled briefly against her, then finally relaxed. Slowly, his sight-less eyes began to focus.

Finally he groaned and sat up. "Ice brother, water sister," he croaked weakly. "The sound — it's really gone?"

"Whatever happened, it's over," Gali assured him. "You're safe now."

Kopaka stretched out a hand to help Lewa to his feet. "What happened, brother?" he asked.

Lewa winced. "Please, Kopaka," he said. "Keep your voice quietlow. My ears are still ringing from the boxing the Kohrak-Kal gave them."

"So it was the Kohrak-Kal," Kopaka said, carefully keeping his voice to little more than a whisper. "Why did it come after you?"

"It didn't, exactly," Lewa admitted, his own voice gaining strength with each passing moment. "It was defending its krana-kal — I had hoped to vineswing down and grab it from above. I thought I was trackfollowing undetected, but I guess it knew I was there after all."

"That was a risky plan, brother," Gali chided him gently.

Kopaka grimaced, his own opinion of Lewa's plan formed of harsher words. But he shrugged them off. Lewa had learned his lesson the hard way.

"What do we do now?" he asked instead. "The more we see of this enemy, the stronger it seems."

"Evertrue, brother," Lewa agreed. "If those swarmqueens are still down there in the dark-tunnels somewhere, it's only a matter of time until the Bohrok-Kal trackfind them."

Kopaka glanced at him, surprised at the normally cheerful Toa Nuva's pessimistic words. "We can't give up," he reminded him. "No matter what, we have to do all we can to protect Mata Nui. It is our destiny."

"I know that everwell, coldbrother," Lewa retorted. "But how does it helpsave Mata Nui to let ourselves be crushed by the Bohrok-Kal? We have tried manyplans, yet nothing can stop them."

Gali cleared her throat. "Wait, brothers," she said quietly. "There is one thing we haven't tried yet. . . ."

THE AGONY OF DEFEAT

"This time I won't stop until I have your krana-kal, monster!" Tahu shouted as he landed atop a ridge just three lengths from the Pahrak-Kal.

The creature paused and glance back toward him. Then it turned away, its bronze-shaded krana-kal seeming to mock him.

"Don't turn your back on me, Pahrak-Kal!" Tahu howled, raising his magma sword and charging after the creature. "I've come for a fight, and a fight I will have!"

The creature merely raised its shield, deflecting Tahu's blows easily. Then it pointed the shield toward the ground. Seconds later, the hardened and cooled magma had melted into a boiling puddle of fresh lava.

Tahu felt himself sinking into the newly created lava puddle. To his surprise, he could feel the burning sensation of the boiling lava on his feet and legs. He leaped backward, landing on the solid ground behind him. Steam rose from his feet.

Uh-oh, he thought in horror. *I didn't realize that my ability to withstand intense heat had deserted me along with my other elemental powers.*

"Are you through with me yet, oh, great Toa?" the Pahrak-Kal taunted.

The creature's scornful tone only fanned the flames of Tahu's anger. "Believe me, when I'm through with you, you won't have to ask."

This time the Pahrak-Kal took a step toward him as it raised its shield. The wave of heat that rippled out from the shield surrounded Tahu, filling his body with searing fire.

Tahu realized all he had to do was fall back again and the heat would stop. All he had to do was retreat. But he couldn't — that would mean letting the Pahrak-Kal win. Giving up.

So this monster wants to fight me with my own element? he thought as the fire filled his body, seeming to burn him up from the inside out. *Fine, then let it do its worst. Better to burn out than to give up. . . .*

"Toa Tahu!" a voice shouted from some-where nearby. Distracted, the Pahrak-Kal turned, at the same time shifting the aim of its shield. Tahu slumped to the ground, gasping at the sudden disappearance of the pain.

As he collapsed, he glanced up and saw Jala, the head of the Ta-Koran guard. Several other Ta-Matoran stood behind him. The Pahrak-Kal watched the newcomers approach.

"Is this your rescue party, Toa?" it hissed with amusement. "They're a little on the puny side."

"Leave us alone, creature!" Jala shouted boldly.

The Pahrak-Kal gazed at the Matoran. "I have no quarrel with any of you, weak ones," it said. "Your hotheaded Toa is the one who wished to test my powers."

With that it turned and moved on along the ridge. Tahu pushed himself to a sitting position as Jala kneeled beside him.

"Are you all right, Toa Tahu?" the Matoran asked with concern.

Tahu pushed aside his helping hand. "I'm fine," he said brusquely, climbing to his feet. "And I'll be even better once I take care of that thing."

"Toa!" Jala cried, grabbing his arm. "Please, stop! You'll get yourself hurt!"

"Better that than living as a coward," Tahu snapped, shaking off the Matoran's grip.

"You have no right!" Jala shouted, anger in his voice.

Tahu stopped short, blinking in surprise. Slowly, he turned to face the Matoran. Jala's eyes behind their mask were defiant.

"What did you say to me?" Tahu asked, holding down his rage with difficulty.

Jala took a deep breath. "I said, you have no right," he said. "You have no right to sacrifice yourself. You have a duty to us — to Mata Nui. Your destiny doesn't allow room for personal pride."

Tahu couldn't help being impressed by the

Matoran's courage in speaking out so boldly. *Of course, it seems like just about everyone is taking things into their own hands lately*, he thought with a flash of annoyance. He had been unpleasantly surprised when he'd first heard that Onua had decided to change plans without consulting him. For a moment he had started to insist on doing things his way — just to make sure that everyone knew who was in charge. But Gali and Pohatu had convinced him that the Earth Toa's decision was right. Was Jala right in his defiance, too?

Out of the corner of his eye, he noticed that the Pahrak-Kal had paused again and seemed to be listening. It took a step back toward them.

"Listen to your little friend, Toa," it hissed with a chuckle. "He's only trying to save you from being humbled by the strength of the Bohrok-Kal. Again."

Tahu gritted his teeth. "Mark my words, Pahrak-Kal," he said slowly, calling upon every ounce of strength he had to control the flames of his temper. "You will not succeed in your mission.

For it is the sworn duty of the Toa Nuva to stop you. And stop you we will."

The Pahrak-Kal laughed, the sound tinny and scornful. "Is that so, feeble hero?" it said. "Once we find and release the queens, you will — *aaaagh!*"

Its words broke off in a strangled cry. To his surprise, Tahu saw that Jala had just leaped forward and wrenched the krana-kal free!

The Pahrak-Kal's limbs twitched, it let out several moans, and then fell still.

"Good job, brave Jala!" Tahu cried with delight. "Now that we've conquered one of them, the others will —"

"Toa Tahu — look!" Another Matoran broke in, pointing to the far end of the ridge.

A Gahlok Va was scuttling toward them. "What's it doing?" Tahu wondered aloud.

He didn't have to wait long for the answer. As the small scout creature came closer, he saw that it was clutching something in its clawed hand.

"Is it — is it bringing the creature another krana-kal?" Jala asked in surprised dismay.

Tahu nodded grimly. "Looks that way."

"Everybody run!" one of the Matoran cried out.

So much for our alliance with the Bohrok and Bohrok Va, Tahu thought hopelessly as he and the Matoran scattered at top speed. *It seems the Bohrok-Kal are exerting some kind of influence over them. It seems we may have made a serious mistake in trusting the swarms inside our villages. . . .*

For a moment, he thought of the Kanohi Vahi. Was this the desperate emergency Vakama had spoken of? Was it time to call upon the dreadful powers of the Great Mask of Time?

He shook his head, feeling helpless and angry as he ran. He could barely control his own temper. Why had Vakama asked him to control such an awesome power?

In the jungle near Le-Koro, Gali was primed for battle. "Ready?" she asked.

Kopaka nodded. "Ready."

"Me, too," Lewa added. "Let's do this."

Gali closed her eyes, gathering and focusing her energy. She concentrated on the other two Toa Nuva, allowing her own mind to flow and merge with theirs. . . .

A moment later, the Toa Nuva Kaita known as Wairuha opened his eyes. Created from the mental and physical uniting of the three Toa, he combined their powers into one form.

"It is time to put an end to this threat," he rumbled, moving toward the Lehvak-Kal that was searching a boggy area nearby.

The Lehvak-Kal stopped what it was doing. "So this is how it will be, Kaita? Then so be it."

As Wairuha moved toward it, the creature let out a series of shrill calls. Seconds later, two more Bohrok-Kal appeared — the Kohrak-Kal and the Gahlok-Kal.

Wairuha gathered his powers. To his surprise, the creatures ignored him and turned instead toward one another. There was a blast of energy — and all of a sudden a single, larger creature stood where three had been a second before!

Wairuha gasped. The Bohrok-Kal had merged into their own Kaita being!

The creature attacked, flinging a solid mass of flickering sound toward him. Wairuha ducked, but it was too late.

The orb caught him and trapped him within an airless, magnetized vortex of sound. Every part of his body was pulled toward every other part by the intense magnetic field, while his mouth gasped for air and his mind shrieked against the pummeling scream of sound.

No, Wairuha thought, struggling to retain consciousness. *Must — fight — against —*

"Oof!" Kopaka grunted as he hit the ground a second later, flung out of the unity by the force of the attack.

Nearby, the Bohrok-Kal Kaita dissolved its own merging, returning to three separate forms. "That was almost — fun," the Lehvak-Kal said with a metallic laugh.

"Yes," the Kohrak-Kal responded. "But we must not think of that. We have to find the queens."

The three creatures turned away from one another and, without further discussion, scuttled off in different directions.

Kopaka watched them go as the strength slowly seeped back into his body. Finally he was able to lift his arms, testing them for injury. "That was *not* fun," he said succinctly.

"Not even a little," Lewa agreed, his voice heavy. "If even the Toa Nuva Kaita can't stand against these creatures, what hope is there?"

Kopaka had to agree with him. No matter how he looked at it, there seemed to be no solution. The Toa Nuva could not stop the Bohrok-Kal — they couldn't even slow them down.

Is this the end? he wondered hopelessly. *Is it our destiny to fall before this unstoppable enemy — to fail in our duty to protect Mata Nui?*

He glanced over at Gali, expecting her to protest against the Air Toa's pessimistic words.

But Gali merely shook her head, her expression downcast. "I fear that at this point, all we can hope is that the creatures' search will turn out to be fruitless," she commented wearily.

"That Cahdok and Gahdok really are gone for good as we had hoped."

Kopaka nodded along with Lewa. But he had his doubts.

In the depths of the earth far below, the waiting dark figure laughed, for he had sensed the Toa's words.

"Giving up so soon, mighty heroes?" he cried with delight, though he knew the Toa could not hear him. "The endless tales and legends of the Turaga surely did not foresee this, did they? But I am not surprised. The Toa may be hailed as heroes, but they are as flawed as any Matoran. Flawed and weak and frightened before this more powerful enemy. And so their story seems to be reaching its end — at last."

The figure glanced over at an enormous mask that stared sightlessly from the cavern wall nearby. He nodded thoughtfully as he gazed at it, his red eyes glowing more brightly than ever.

"Fear not, brother," he said. "As long as I am here, nothing will ever disturb you. . . ."

A NEW HOPE

"Are you two going to tell me what this is about?" Tahu Nuva asked.

Pohatu Nuva could tell that the Fire Toa was reaching the end of his meager store of patience. "Soon, brother," he said soothingly. "It will be easier to discuss it when we're all together."

Onua, who was in the lead, glanced over his shoulder and nodded. "A Matoran told us he saw Gali, Lewa, and Kopaka here in the jungle. We should be with them shortly."

Tahu sighed loudly, but didn't protest further. Pohatu was relieved. If what he and Onua had just learned was true, the Toa Nuva had much more important things to do than bicker among themselves.

Soon they heard voices through the trees,

and a moment later the other three Toa Nuva emerged in a clearing. Gali spotted them first.

"Brothers!" she called, hurrying toward them. "We were just talking about coming to find you. We've had a rather disturbing experience that we thought you should hear about."

"You're not the only ones," Pohatu replied. "Wait until you hear what Onua and I found out."

"Yes," Tahu said irritably. "I *have* been waiting for that. Too long."

Onua nodded at Gali and the other two Toa Nuva who had just hurried up behind her. "Why don't you three go first?" he suggested.

"Well, it all began with Gali's ideaplan," Lewa said. "See, she and Kopaka had just helpfound me after I had a tangle with the Kohrak-Kal, and —"

"Why don't we try the short version of the story?" Kopaka interrupted. "We merged into Wairuha. Three Bohrok-Kal formed their own Kaita. They beat us."

Lewa rolled his eyes. "Some storyteller you are," he muttered.

Pohatu hardly heard him. He was too shocked by what Kopaka had just said. "The Toa Nuva Kaita," he exclaimed. "And it was no match for the Bohrok-Kal?"

"Not even close," Gali admitted. "Its power — it was astonishing. It disunited us, leaving us helpless. Fortunately it seemed to have no interest in fighting us further and left — heading toward the north."

"We might know why it went that way," Onua said heavily. "Come, let's walk that direction ourselves as we talk — you'll understand why in a moment. Pohatu, why don't you tell them what we learned?"

Pohatu nodded. "With all due respect to brother Kopaka, I think I'll tell the medium-length version of the story," he said.

He went on to describe how he and Onua had tracked the Tahnok-Kal to the beach on the eastern shore of the island. They had hidden in the woods nearby and concocted a plan to disable it by reflecting its lightning bolts back over its head toward a tall tree behind the creature.

For once, the plan had worked perfectly, and the tree had cracked and fallen right on the Tahnok-Kal, trapping it. The two Toa Nuva had been able to remove the krana-kal from the creature with little trouble.

"Then the krana-kal spoke to us," Pohatu continued. "It told us we were already too late — that the Bohrok-Kal had learned where Cahdok and Gahdok were trapped."

Lewa gasped. "But we were so sure that the swarmqueens were no more," he exclaimed.

"We mentioned that to the krana-kal," Onua said wryly. "It seemed quite convinced that we were wrong."

Pohatu nodded. "The Bohrok swarms have left the villages where they were working. All of them seem to be heading back to their nest — as if obeying a command."

Onua nodded. "If we're to have any hope of protecting Mata Nui, we've got to get there before them," he said. "That's why we're heading north — to Po-Wahi."

By this time the group had reached the

edge of the jungle. "So we're going back to the tunnel entrance?" Gali asked. "But we've already been there. The tunnel was filled in with rocks."

"Yes, we know," Pohatu said. "But we have most of our Kanohi Nuva now. We might be able to push through somehow, or dig a shortcut into the lair. Just so long as we get down there before the Bohrok-Kal find their way underground."

"What good will that do?" Lewa asked, vaulting over a low wall of tumbled stones. "Don't you think they can easywin belowground as well as above it?"

Kopaka was looking thoughtful. "I know," he spoke up. "The Exo-Toa."

"That's right," Pohatu said. "We don't have our powers, but the Exo-Toa armor will give us strength if we can reach them in time."

The others nodded. They all remembered the giant suits of armor that they had encountered underground. The Exo-Toa armor had helped them trap Cahdok and Gahdok. The last they had seen it, it was still there near the Bahrag's lair.

There was little conversation as the group continued across the plains and deserts of Po-Wahi, each deep in his or her own thoughts.

Finally they reached the base of the hill leading to the cave entrance. "Almost there," Tahu commented. He led the way up the slope.

A moment later all six Toa Nuva stopped short, staring in surprise at the sight before them. The huge pile of rocks that had covered the entrance the last time they'd seen it was gone — completely melted. The entrance yawned open, leading down into the darkness.

11

TAHU'S DECISION

Kopaka glanced toward the hole in the floor of the underground chamber. How long had it been since Lewa had levitated down through it?

To distract himself, he looked around the underground chamber. It hadn't changed much since the last time he had seen it, just after the defeat of the Bahrag. The only real difference was the jagged hole burned into the floor.

Onua was standing near the hole, his head tipped to one side. "Do you hear something?"

Gali smiled. "None of us have the sensitive hearing you do, brother," she reminded him. "What do you hear?"

"I'm not sure." Onua frowned, leaning closer to the hole. "Strange, faraway sounds —

like shattering glass or stone. I hope Lewa is okay. Maybe we shouldn't have let him go down alone."

"He is the best of all of us at moving quickly and silently," Pohatu reminded him. "Anyway, if he doesn't return soon, we can —"

"Everbad sightnews!" Lewa said, popping up out of the hole so suddenly that the waiting Toa Nuva all jumped in surprise. He sounded breathless, and his eyes were wide and worried. "The Bohrok-Kal are downcave, all right. They're groupstanding cubefront with their iconloot, and the hardluck Exo-Toa is downfalling everquick, and —"

"Wait!" Onua cut him off. "Brother, slow down. What are you telling us?"

Lewa took a deep breath. "Truesorry," he said. "It's just that what I saw was so scarybad. The Exo-Toa — they were watchguarding the Bahrag's prison. By themselves."

Kopaka blinked in surprise. The suits of armor — they could act on their own?

"Are you sure?" he asked Lewa.

"Truesure," Lewa replied. "They were fight-

74

ing against the Bohrok-Kal — but having sorry-bad luck at it. I saw the creatures destroy most of the Exo-Toa before I hurryleft to come back."

Gali's eyes were somber. "I see," she said. "What was that you said about a cube?"

"Oh!" Lewa said quickly. "There was a cube — a lightglowing, airhovering thing. It was in front of the darkcavern. I couldn't see what was inside the cavern. But I can dreadguess."

"Cahdok and Gahdok," Pohatu said solemnly, voicing what all were thinking.

Lewa nodded. "The cube had shapecarved spaces on each side," he said. "A perfect fit for the power symbols that were stolen from us."

"That must be why the Bohrok-Kal wanted the icons," Onua said, his eyes lighting up with realization. "They must need to fit them into that cube in order to release the Bahrag — it's like a lock of some kind."

"This is bad," Kopaka said. "We'd better get down there and do whatever we can to stop them."

"How?" Pohatu wondered. "We still don't

have our powers. It sounds like we don't even have the Exo-Toa option anymore. All we have is a few paltry mask powers."

"Yes, a few mask powers," Gali said. "And our wits. And our duty."

Tahu strode toward the hole. "And that will have to be enough."

A few paltry mask powers, Tahu thought as he levitated down the long, dark tunnel. *If the others only knew about the not-so-paltry mask power I hold — but is now finally the time to reveal it?*

He thought back to that moment in the suva in Ta-Koro. He could almost hear Vakama's solemn words echoing in his head. *He who controls time controls reality — controls everything.*

Tahu grimaced. Was he ready to control everything? Could anyone ever be truly ready for that — even a powerful Toa Nuva?

Tahu slowed his descent as the lower cavern came into view. All six of the Bohrok-Kal were there, gathered around the floating cube. What was left of the Exo-Toa lay scattered on the stone floor nearby — most of the suits had been pulled to pieces.

"There must be something we can do," Gali said.

Tahu took a deep breath, suddenly feeling in his heart that the decision was already made. It had been destined — all he had to do was accept it.

"There is," he said.

THE GREAT MASK OF TIME

Gali glanced at Tahu, wondering what the Fire Toa had in mind. She gasped as she saw his mask begin to glow a fiery orange and morph into an odd, primitive shape.

"Tahu!" she exclaimed. "What are you doing?"

"Something I hoped I would never have to do," Tahu replied hollowly. "Something that could mean the end of everything. I call upon — the Great Mask of Time!"

Gali felt her heart constrict with terror. "Then you may have doomed us all," she whispered bleakly.

She was distracted by an echoing voice drifting up from the cavern below. "Free us, my children!" it wailed joyfully.

"Yes!" a second voice joined the first. "Unlock this prison, my children, and set us free!"

"The Bohrok queens," Tahu said. "I'm going in."

Without waiting for agreement, he levitated downward. Gali followed along with the other Toa. Soon she was low enough to see into the cavern beyond the cube, where the enormous, monstrous forms of Cahdok and Gahdok were barely visible beyond a hazy wall.

The Bahrag soon spotted the Toa Nuva as well. "You are too late!" Cahdok howled, her words slightly garbled by the mass of protodermis that was holding her hostage.

As her feet touched the stone floor, Gali glanced worriedly at Tahu. He was standing beside her, his head bowed in concentration.

"Gali, I must use this power," he said. "I must master it — or all is lost."

"But if you fail," she said urgently, "Mata Nui will fall. All of reality may be undone!"

The Vahi glowed brightly. "Then I will not fail," Tahu said grimly.

Gali held her breath as a ripple of energy radiated out from Tahu's mask. The air seemed to quiver as the time energy moved through it.

The Vahi's energy struck the Bohrok-Kal just as they raised their clawed arms to move the icons into place. Their movements slowed more and more, until the motion was barely perceptible.

"It's working!" Onua cried in relief.

For a moment, Gali shared his joy. Then she glanced at Tahu. His hands were clenched into fists, and every muscle of his body quivered uncontrollably.

"I can't . . . hold back time . . . much longer!" Tahu gasped, his voice twisted with exertion. "Go! Get our symbols back!"

The other five Toa Nuva leaped forward as one. As Gali headed toward the Nuhvok-Kal, she could see its krana-kal. Despite the time slowdown, it still appeared to be pulsing evenly.

Gali paused, staring at it as it shimmered and glowed. Was the time mutation playing tricks with her eyes, or was it — changing?

"Hold on," she said to the others. "Something's happening. Their krana-kal are changing — turning silver."

Kopaka moved forward for a better look. He was stopped a short distance away, as if he'd just run into a wall. "A field of energy surrounds them," he said grimly. "In the final moments before they complete their task, they must be protected from all harm. Even the slowing of time could not stop it."

"Forgive me if I test your theory," Onua said, hurling the chunk of stone at the Bohrok-Kal with all his might.

ZZZZZZZZZK!

The stone struck the force field and disintegrated. Gali shook her head worriedly as she glanced at Tahu, who was still shaking with the effort to control the Great Mask of Time.

Lewa shuddered. "It's over," he said. "Even when we still had our powers, we were barely able to fightsnare the Bahrag at their ordinary strength. We've failed. Failed our villages, our people . . ."

For once, words seemed to desert the Air Toa, and he merely shook his head to complete his point. Gali glanced around the group. The other Toa Nuva looked just as dejected as Lewa. Onua was staring in disbelief at the spot where the stone had disintegrated. Nearby, Pohatu was shifting his weight nervously from one foot to the other. Kopaka said nothing as usual, staring fixedly at the Bahrag in their glutinous cage. And for the first time since she'd known him, Gali saw defeat lurking in Tahu's eyes.

But Gali herself was not yet ready to give up. Unity — duty — destiny — so far, the Matoran creed had never failed them.

"Remember," she said thoughtfully, "we have always had the most success when we have been willing to dig deep inside our hearts and risk *everything* — even our very selves. . . ."

THE POWER WITHIN

The other Toa stared at Gali, confused. "What do you mean?" Pohatu asked her.

"Our powers!" Gali explained, her eyes lighting with hope. "If the essence of our powers is housed in those symbols, maybe we can use that against the Bohrok-Kal!"

Tahu stared at her as the power of the Vahi began to waver and weaken. Tahu himself was weakening, also. "How?" he asked, pushing out the single word with effort.

"We need to pool our willpower," Gali said. "Reach out to our symbols. Even if it means freeing the Bohrok-Kal from the Vahi."

Tahu shook his head, not understanding. He was tired — so tired. Perhaps it was time to give up, to allow the Vahi to overwhelm him . . .

"Tahu!" Kopaka said sharply. "The mask. You have to send it away — now."

The Ice Toa's voice was always enough to set Tahu on edge. Now it broke through the haze in his mind. *Who is he to tell me what to do?*

But Kopaka was right. The Vahi had served its purpose.

"Vahi," he croaked. "Be gone!"

He nearly collapsed as the intense time power released him and the Vahi faded. Pohatu reached forward to catch him. "Easy, brother," the Stone Toa said. "There you go. Now come on, pull yourself together — we have work to do."

Tahu nodded, pulling in a deep breath. "I am ready," he said.

The Bohrok-Kal, released from the power of the Vahi, were beginning to stir. "Hurry," Onua said urgently. "We don't have much time."

The Toa Nuva turned to face the cube. Tahu could already feel his strength flowing back into him. He gathered that energy, pushing it outward toward the power symbols. Around him, he could feel the other Toa Nuva doing the same.

Tahu had never felt such an intense wave of energy. But would it work? Would their combined power stop the Bohrok-Kal? A glow surrounded the Toa, growing brighter with every passing second. Slowly, the glow took separate form, moving forward toward the Bohrok-Kal.

It neared the force field surrounding the Bohrok-Kal, which their krana-kal were still holding steady. "Concentrate!" Tahu urged the others. "We must break through!"

He could see that the power symbols were beginning to glow in response to the Toa Nuva's energy. The glow pulsed outward, surrounding the Bohrok-Kal.

"What is happening?" the Nuhvok-Kal said in its metallic voice. "I feel stronger! The Toa Nuva symbols are feeding us energy!"

I hope this works, Tahu thought, as the Bohrok-Kal all pulled the icons back from the cube, gazing at them in wonder. *If not, we might have given the enemy even more power than it already had. . . .*

The Lehvak-Kal held up its icon. "Yes!" it

said. "Cahdok and Gahdok do not need the swarms — with this power, we can return Mata Nui to the Before-Time."

"No!" Gahdok howled. "My children, do not be distracted from your task!"

But the Bohrok-Kal seemed not to hear her. "We will rule beside the Bahrag!" the Gahlok-Kal cried, its body pulsing. "We will —" It shuddered, the energy turning darker.

"What is happening?" the Tahnok-Kal wailed as its body quivered uncontrollably, waves of energy rippling and sparking over it.

"Good question," Pohatu whispered.

The Bohrok-Kal were all convulsing by now. "No!" the Gahlok-Kal shrieked as its body lurched. "Too much power — can't control!"

"You fools!" Cahdok roared from within her prison. "You have been tricked!"

"Yes," Gali said calmly from the head of the group. "You wanted our power, monsters. Now let us see if you can handle it!"

The Nuhvok-Kal dropped the symbol it was holding.

"So much power," the Nuhvok-Kal moaned. "Can't control my energies . . . Gravity crushing me . . ."

Tahu gasped as the Nuhvok-Kal's powerful body began to crumple and fold in upon itself. "He's throwing out an uncontrolled gravity field — it's going to crush him!"

"Bahrag, aid us!" the Nuhvok-Kal pleaded, its voice distorted by the weight crushing down on it. "Before it is too laaaaaaate . . ."

The last word trailed off into nothingness. The gravitational force had finally overwhelmed it, compressing the creature into a miniature black hole in the middle of the chamber.

Lewa gasped. "It's awaygone!" he murmured in amazement.

Tahu didn't respond. He was watching the Pahrak-Kal, which was struggling against its own power overload. It had hurled its Toa Nuva icon away, but it was too late. The Pahrak-Kal's armored body was glowing with a plasma-fueled heat so intense that the stone floor started to melt beneath its feet.

"I will contain this power!" The Pahrak-Kal sounded drippy and slow, as if it, too, were melting. "I am Pahrak-Kal! I cannot be defeated!"

But a moment later, the floor beneath the Pahrak-Kal gave way entirely, and the creature dropped away through it out of sight.

Tahu glanced toward the cube just in time to see the Gahlok-Kal stepping toward it, one of the power icons still clutched in its hand. "Uh-oh," Tahu said, pointing.

"The Bahrag will be free!" the Gahlok-Kal cried. "You cannot defeat me with my own power!"

"Should we do something?" Lewa wondered aloud.

Tahu shook his head. "One symbol will not free the Bahrag," he said. "It would need to collect all six of them. And I suspect that's going to be harder than it realizes. . . ."

At that moment they all became aware that the pieces of shattered Exo-Toa armor were moving. "Look!" Gali said. "It's the Gahlok-Kal's magnetic energy. It's going to —"

Before she could finish the sentence, the Exo-Toa pieces suddenly shot toward the Gahlok-Kal, pulled there by the creature's pulsing magnetic force.

"Oh, no!" the Gahlok-Kal cried, a split second before the pieces struck.

Tahu had turned to watch the Lehvak-Kal. The incredible vacuum forces it was emitting finally overwhelmed it, sending it shooting upward like a rocket. It smashed through the cavern ceiling and disappeared.

The Tahnok-Kal had teetered over to a corner of the cave. There, it stood locked into place, a prisoner of its own electrical forces, which swirled in the air around it and formed a constant shimmer of concentrated lightning.

Onua nodded toward the helpless creature. "I expect that one will stay there until it finally runs out of energy entirely."

That meant the only Bohrok-Kal left was the Kohrak-Kal. It was standing near the cube, buffeted by waves of undiluted sound. The sonic forces were so focused around their core that

Tahu could hear nothing but faint *zips* and *kreeees*. But he shuddered to imagine what it must sound like to the creature trapped within its own sonic vortex.

As he watched, the Kohrak-Kal's body shuddered and gave way to the pressure, crumbling into dust before the pummeling sound waves. Only its silvery krana-kal escaped, scuttling away into the shadows.

The six power symbols lay on the floor. Slowly, the glow that had surrounded them faded away, and the cavern was still.

Lewa let out a long breath. "The Bohrok-Kal," he said. "Are they . . . ?"

"They did not live as we understand life, so they cannot die," Kopaka answered. "But they have been defeated."

Tahu nodded. "Did you see that krana-kal escaping?" he asked.

"I did," Gali said. "I expect the others managed to get away, too. But I don't think we need to worry. Without the Bohrok-Kal to house them, the krana-kal will remain powerless."

"Then we have won!" Tahu said, hardly daring to believe it.

Kopaka nodded. "It seems so," he said, his cool voice tinged with admiration. "Thanks to our wise sister. How did you know, Gali?"

Gali shrugged. "I didn't," she admitted. "I gambled that tapping the power of the symbols would feed the Bohrok-Kal more energy than they could control. In the end, the only power that could defeat them was their own." She turned toward Tahu. "There's one thing I don't understand," she said. "The Vahi — where did you get it?"

"Vakama gave it to me," Tahu said. "Along with a warning — that its power might be too great for even a Toa to wield. He was nearly right."

As he remembered the surge of power that the Vahi had sent through him, a surge of energy welled up. He held up his sword, seeing flames dancing along its length. Hardly daring to believe what he saw, he pointed the sword at a nearby rock, blasting it with searing flames.

Kopaka was watching him. "So our powers have returned," he said. Glancing toward the cavern ceiling, he pointed his own ice blade. A moment later an icy staircase had formed.

Tahu led the other Toa Nuva toward the icy staircase. The Bahrag were once again safely contained in their underground prison. It was time for the Toa Nuva to return to the surface.

None of the Toa Nuva could relax before the first rays of sun penetrated the dark tunnel — a sign they were at last reaching the surface.

Once safely above, the six Toa sank to the ground in relief. Gali glanced at Tahu with unease, still trying to process what he had just revealed — still trying to understand how he had kept the Great Mask of Time a secret for so long. What other secrets might he be hiding?

But she suppressed her unease — now was not the time. Instead, forcing a smile, she turned to her fellow Toa Nuva and said, "Well, brothers, what do you think? Will we be able to put Mata Nui right again?"

"Of course," Tahu said. "I think we've finally learned our lesson."

"What lesson?" Lewa said. "You mean the lesson that a Toa's work is never done?"

Pohatu chuckled. "No, he's probably talking about the lesson that we should always pay attention to Gali's hunches."

"Or that only bad-yuck things happen underground," Lewa added, grinning.

"Yes, all of those lessons, brothers," Tahu said with a smile. "But also the most important one of all. Don't you get it?"

"I know what you're thinking, brother," Gali said, hoping she was right. "Three little words, right?"

Kopaka nodded, speaking up for the first time since Tahu's speech had ended. "Unity, duty, destiny," he said.

"Right," Tahu said. "When we keep those three words in mind, the Toa Nuva can do *anything*!"